D0387144

PICO BRANCH
Santa Monica Public Library      NOV _ _ 2017

# HORRIBLE HARRY
## and the Field Day Revenge

# Other Books by Suzy Kline

# HORRIBLE HARRY
## and the Field Day Revenge

BY **SUZY KLINE**

PICTURES BY **AMY WUMMER**

**VIKING**

VIKING
Penguin Young Readers Group
An imprint of Penguin Random House LLC
375 Hudson Street
New York, New York 10014

First published in the United States of America by Viking, an imprint of
Penguin Random House LLC, 2017

Text copyright © 2017 by Suzy Kline
Illustrations copyright © 2017 by Penguin Random House LLC

Penguin supports copyright. Copyright fuels creativity, encourages diverse
voices, promotes free speech, and creates a vibrant culture. Thank you for
buying an authorized edition of this book and for complying with copyright
laws by not reproducing, scanning, or distributing any part of it in any form
without permission. You are supporting writers and allowing Penguin to
continue to publish books for every reader.

LIBRARY OF CONGRESS CATALOGING-IN-PUBLICATION DATA IS AVAILABLE
ISBN 9780425290361

Manufactured in China

1 3 5 7 9 10 8 6 4 2

## DEDICATED TO

*my five precious grandchildren who*
*love to play outdoor games:*
*Jake, Kenna, Gabby, Saylor, and Holden*

## Acknowledgments

Heartfelt thanks to the dedicated phys ed staff at Brookside Elementary School in Ossining, New York, for their wonderful field day information, and to the nine-year-old boy there who ran the two-hundred-yard dash in thirty-seven seconds!

And many thanks to Victor for his excellent help with the jump roping, the tug-of-war contest, and Harry's second original riddle.

Special appreciation for my hardworking editor, Margaret Rosenthal, whose encouragement and outstanding editorial work helped me greatly with this book.

And for Rufus for all his support and love.

# Contents

# The Box

Field Day is supposed to be fun. You get to play all kinds of games outdoors and cheer for your team.

But this year, in third grade?

Field Day turned into a war of trouble and *revenge*.

It all started yesterday morning with a box. A big brown box.

Our teacher, Mrs. Flaubert (who used to be Miss Mackle before she got married), dropped us off for gym class. "Please go to your spots," she said, "and wait for Mr. Deltoid."

Spots are colored places on our gym floor about the size of a Frisbee. We each have one. My friend Harry, who likes to do crazy horrible things, raced down the ramp as usual to his yellow spot. He jumped high in the air like he was dunking a basket. Ida leaped and twirled around Harry until she did a final pirouette on her space.

Mary placed her feet on her red spot perfectly so both sneakers fit inside. As soon as Song Lee and Sidney got to their spots, Mary glanced at the wall clock.

"Hey, Doug," she said. "Looks like Mr. Deltoid is late again. I bet he's getting coffee in the cafeteria."

"And a cookie," I added. "It's that time of morning when Mrs. Funderburke is baking. Can you smell chocolate?"

"Yes!" Mary said, taking a deep whiff. "Chocolate chip cookies are on our lunch menu."

When Mary giggled, I did too.

Mrs. Flaubert was waiting at the top of the ramp. She was *not* giggling.

"Harry!" she called out. "No headstands!"

Harry did a somersault instead.

"Harry Spooger!" our teacher snapped. "You need a mat for that!"

"You'll break your back," Mary added.

"Just warming up for Field

4

Day tomorrow!" he said, racing in place.

Mrs. Flaubert folded her arms and waited for Mr. Deltoid.

Finally, he showed up, four minutes late. There was a chocolatey smudge near the corner of his lip, and a coffee stain on his gray sweatshirt.

Mary and I put two thumbs up.

Our teacher gave the gym teacher a quick nod, then took off.

"Hey, boys and girls!" Mr. Deltoid exclaimed as he jogged down the ramp. "I've got the biggest news for you!"

We all listened up.

"Tomorrow, as you know, is South School's Field Day."

Mr. Deltoid danced over to the gym supply closet and opened the door. "*This year*, each class will have two Field Day winners. These lucky winners get to open up this . . ."

And then he disappeared into his supply closet.

No one moved. Not even Harry.

"Ta-da!" he said popping out of that little room.

He was holding up a big brown box. There was nothing on it except for a long piece of masking tape that went over the top. We had no clue what was inside.

When Mr. Deltoid dropped the box, it landed with a thud on the gym floor.

"This is packed with Field Day

prizes," he said. Lots of us cheered, but Harry was the loudest.

Our gym teacher continued, "First place in any event wins three points, second place earns two, and third place one. Anyone who displays bad sportsmanship will lose a point, so remember that when you think of firing a bean bag at someone."

After we laughed, Mr. Deltoid added, "The partner team with the highest score will get to choose Room 3B's gift out of this box." Then he tapped it like a drum.

"Can we pick partners now?" ZuZu asked.

I immediately looked over at Harry. I wanted to be his partner. He was pointing at me and flashing his white teeth.

"Yes," the gym teacher answered, "but we'll do it by drawing names out of a jar. It's good to mix things up! There's always a little luck in every sports event, *and* it's good to work with different people!"

Harry immediately made prayer hands. It *would* take a miracle!

Our class had twenty kids, which meant the odds were against us!

I made prayer hands too.

# Pickle Jar Picks

While we took four laps around the gym, Mr. Deltoid quickly cut up our class list. It had our names on it in large bold print. He scooped up the strips of paper and dropped them into his big plastic jar. It had a picture of a green dill pickle on the front.

Harry finished his laps first easily. Dexter and I tied for second. ZuZu, Song Lee, Sid, and Ida weren't far behind us. Mary was last as usual.

As soon as she rounded that fourth lap, Mr. Deltoid called us over. "Okay, guys, let's get started. If I call your name, come up and pick your partner out of the pickle jar. That's fair and square!"

*Not fair*, I thought. *Harry and I haven't been partners all year. Last time, I got bossy Mary for a bug partner!*

Our gym teacher picked the first name out of the jar. "Sidney!" he called. Sid hurried over.

"I like . . . being . . . first!" he said, a little out of breath. He swished his hand inside the big pickle jar and pulled out a name. "IDA!" he yelled.

Ida skipped over to Sid and slapped him five. Those two played jump rope a lot together at recess.

Mr. Deltoid pointed to a bin of white T-shirts. "The PTA has donated these for tomorrow's Field Day, so take one and go over to the side tables. There are special Magic Markers there along with scratch paper, pens, and rulers. Come up with a good name for your team and get busy designing your T-shirts."

Mr. Deltoid picked again. "ZuZu!"

ZuZu ran over and pulled a paper strip from the pickle jar. "Dexter!" he cheered.

Dexter pretended to strum a guitar like Elvis. "Dude!" he sang out. *"I'm all shook up!"*

They were going to be a tough combo to beat.

Harry moved his prayer hands up to his lips.

"Song Lee!" the teacher hollered.

Song Lee hurried over and reached into the jar. "Mary!" she said with a big smile.

Both girls joined hands and skipped away.

When it was Harry's turn, he flew up to the pickle jar with outstretched arms, then yanked out a paper strip. He had the wrong side so he turned it over.

After staring at it for a long moment, he screamed, "DOUGO!"

Everyone laughed. Harry is the only one who calls me that. I couldn't believe it! It was a miracle! Harry and I leaped in the air!

"I'm so psyched!" I said. "This *never* happens!"

"I know," Harry said as we walked over to the T-shirt bin. "I had to do something about it."

I immediately stopped in my

tracks. "What do you mean . . . Harry?"

He smiled ear to ear. "I got lucky!"

"How?" I said. Harry showed me his strip of paper.

Both sides were blank.

My eyes bulged.

When I heard my name being called again, I slowly turned around. There were just a few other kids left.

"Harry must have dropped Doug's name back into the jar," the teacher guessed. "Let's pick a different name."

Whoa . . . I was *so* relieved.

"Come on, Dougo," Harry said, "we need a name for our team." We grabbed our tees and found a place at one of the two long art tables.

For the next forty-five minutes, we all designed our T-shirts at the tables in the gym.

Harry came up with the name for our team: the Speedy Spiders!

Actually, spiders give me the willies, but Harry loves creepy creatures. He even had a pet spider once, Charles. Their webs are awesome, though, so I agreed and started making one with a ruler.

Twenty minutes later, I checked out the competition. Song Lee and Mary made T-shirts with flying birds. Their rainbow wings were really cool.

ZuZu and Dexter were the Rockin'

Dudes. They drew two guys with Elvis hairdos dashing to the finish line.

Sidney and Ida were the Star Jumpers. They had bright orange and yel-low stars outlined in black all over their shirts.

If I stood up, I could see more at the far table. The best team name there was—the Dashing Doorknobs.

Harry leaned over and whispered, "We're going to win tomorrow, Dougo."

"I hope so!" I replied. "Just no more fast ones, Harry. We were lucky not to get in trouble."

I had no idea *then* that Harry's pickle jar trick was about to backfire.

# The Backfire

As soon as the clock turned eleven, Mrs. Flaubert appeared on the ramp. She was smiling again.

"Line up, kids!" Mr. Deltoid roared. "Harry and Doug, stay put." His hand was resting on Harry's shoulder. "We need to talk," he said softly.

*Uh-oh*, I thought.

Mr. Deltoid had a quick word with our teacher before she left. Then he joined our table. "So, do you boys want to tell me anything?" he asked.

I said nothing. I couldn't tattle on my buddy.

"I can't wait for tomorrow, Mr. Deltoid!" Harry said with a jack-o'-lantern grin.

Mr. Deltoid lowered his eyebrows. "Nothing about the partner drawing?"

Harry looked into Mr. Deltoid's dark probing eyes. He was cornered. Very slowly, he reached into his pocket and pulled out his blank strip of paper.

"It was like getting a Chance card in Monopoly," Harry confessed. "There wasn't a name on it, so I read it as Doug. We haven't been partners all year. Not even once!"

"So you thought it was a *Pick Your Own Partner Card*?"

"Yes, Mr. Deltoid," Harry said. "Sorry."

"I'm sorry too," I blurted out.

"Well, the partners came out even. And apparently, I did include one blank. But you should have acknowledged it instead of trying to sneak it by me."

Harry nodded. "You're right. I won't do it again!"

Mr. Deltoid got up. "Okay," he said, tapping the table. "We'll leave it as it is. The T-shirts are already designed. But there is a consequence! You two are cleaning up this mess. Sponges and spray bottles are in the closet. I want every streak off these tables, and everything put away!"

"Absolutely!" Harry replied, standing up like a soldier and saluting him.

"We're on it! Right, Doug?"

"Right!" I agreed, then immediately picked up a green marker off the floor and dropped it into the tin can.

"When I return," Mr. Deltoid added as he walked up the ramp, "I expect to find your work done, and done well."

I knew where *he* was going.

To the cafeteria, which was on the same basement floor as the gym. He wanted another warm cookie.

It didn't take us long to gather up all the Magic Markers and get them back in the tins. Harry rubbed and scrubbed the colorful streaks off one table, and I wiped down the other. "No more marks," I said proudly.

"Great! I'll put the markers away," Harry said, and he carried the tins into the open supply closet.

When he didn't come out right away, I started to wonder what he was doing in there. After a minute or so, I decided to check on him. "What's taking you so . . ."

My eyes felt like they'd popped out of my sockets.

"HARRY! *What* are you doing?"

# Sneak and Peek!

Harry's fingers were peeling the masking tape off that big box of prizes! "Stop!" I said. "You'll get in BIG trouble! Me too!"

Harry held up a hand. "Just peeking, Dougo. I'm not taking anything. I *never* steal. Just peeking . . ."

Harry peeled off the rest of the tape and attached it to a shelf. "Look!" he said. "It's a dangling rattlesnake. Cool, huh?"

None of this was cool to me. It was horrible!

Harry opened up the two flaps and looked inside at all the prizes. "Boring, boring, boring . . ." he groaned.

Then . . . he spied something at the bottom. "Oh man . . . you *have* to see this, Dougo! It's the *perfect* prize for Room 3B! Everyone will love it!"

I covered my eyes. "I don't want to know what it is!"

I ducked outside and glanced up at the ramp. "Mr. Deltoid will be coming soon!" I called out.

When I peeked in on Harry again, he was putting the flaps back down on the box and reaching for that snakelike tape.

"We have to win tomorrow, Dougo!" Harry said, smoothing the sticky strip across the top of the box. "We have to be the ones to pick Room 3B's prize!"

Suddenly, I heard footsteps approaching the ramp. "Mr. Deltoid's *coming!*" I warned.

Seconds later, Harry jumped out of the supply closet like Superman. "Done!" he said, grabbing our tees off the table and tossing me mine. "Let's go meet him!"

As we hurried across the gym, I whispered, "Don't tell me what you saw in that Field Day box."

"Your call!" Harry said. "Just look forward to a cool surprise!"

"Hey, boys!" Mr. Deltoid boomed. "Let's see how well you cleaned up."

*Oh man*, I thought. Did Harry leave the box exactly where he found it? Was the tape on good enough?

We watched while Mr. Deltoid checked the tables then walked into his supply cabinet.

One goof, and Mr. Deltoid would know someone was messing with his stuff. "Nice job, guys," he finally said.

"Thanks!" Harry replied.

I exhaled deeply. *Phew!* I thought.

At last, we headed upstairs to

Room 3B.

"We've been lucky twice now, Harry!" I said. "No more crazy stuff! Okay?"

"Okay!" Harry agreed.

I hoped he meant it. Being Harry's partner was like walking on the edge of a cliff!

I had to keep a close watch at all times!

# A Big Fat Cheater?

The next morning when I arrived at South School, there were five flagged event areas: jump roping, water brigade, bean bag toss, two-man relay, and tug-of-war.

Each had a colorful pennant. A big banner was hung from the second-floor windows. It said SOUTH SCHOOL FIELD DAY. Two events this year were in the new nature area. I couldn't wait for those!

Our class started with the jump rope

contest on the playground. Harry was wearing his T-shirt with a dozen spiders running across it. Mine had a big web on the front and the words SPEEDY SPIDERS on the back.

"Awesome shoes!" I said, admiring the big spider drawn on each of Harry's sneakers.

"Thanks!" he answered. "Want me to make a spider on yours?"

"No. That would creep me out," I said.

Harry just laughed.

The music teacher and our school nurse were waiting for us on the black-top. Mr. Marks greeted us with a tune from *Hello, Dolly!*

"Hello, jumpers! Well, hello, jumpers . . ." he sang out. He was standing next to a huge pile of plastic jump ropes.

"Please make your selection!"

I picked a chartreuse one. Harry took a red-and-white rope.

"The jumper who lasts the longest wins three points for his or her team!" Mr. Marks explained.

Mrs. Cherry got us started. "Okay, boys and girls, get your jump ropes ready. Make sure you have enough space."

We all found a comfortable spot. I moved next to Mary where there was plenty of room.

"All set?" the nurse asked.

"YES!" everyone answered.

"*GO!*" she called out.

I started jumping. Each time I landed on my tiptoes, I quickly hopped again over my rope. I kept spinning my wrists

around and around until I got into a rhythm. Dexter was in his own world, jumping to the tune of an Elvis song. I could hear him singing, "You ain't nothin' but a hound dog . . ." softly to himself.

One minute later, eight people were sitting on the sidelines watching the jump rope contest.

My legs started to get tired, and my calves were tightening up. But I kept jumping!

Mary and Song Lee were in perfect unison. Sid and Ida were too. They were the varsity squad of jumpers!

After two very long minutes, Harry broke his silence. "Hey," he called out, "did anyone hear the joke about the two cannonballs that got married?"

Mary answered right away. "That's

old, Harry Spooger! They had a little beebeeeeeeee." Then, as she glared at Harry, she lost sight of the rope and tripped up!

Boy, was Mary mad! She dragged her rope to the sidelines, mumbling, "Harry Spooger is *a big fat cheater*!"

I don't think anyone else heard her.

"Hey, guys," Harry continued, "I just made up a new one! Did you hear about the *two baseballs* that got married?"

"No," Sid replied while his rope smacked the pavement with a steady beat. "What happened?"

"They went looking for a diamond!"

Sid started laughing, lost his rhythm,

and stumbled over his rope. Sidney LaFleur was out!

*Oh man*, I wondered. Was it really true? Was Harry a big fat cheater? Suddenly, I toppled over my own rope just thinking about it!

Now *I* was out. I started to know how Sid must feel. I sat next to him. Harry's jokes didn't trip me up, though, my worrying did!

"Tough luck, Dougo!" Harry yelled.

Mr. Marks counted the people who were still jumping as he wheeled in an Igloo of bottled waters.

There were three jumpers left—Harry, Song Lee, and Ida.

Sidney was sitting next to Mary on the sidelines. They both were frowning.

"Have another riddle?" Ida asked

Harry as she kept flipping the rope over her head.

Harry turned to answer, lost his footing, and went down to the ground.

Boy, did Mary and Sidney do silent cheers!

"Sorry," Ida replied, and then she lost her steady beat and slipped up too.

"Game over! Super job, kids!" Mr. Marks called from the far sideline. "Song Lee is our champion. Ida is second, and Harry is third."

The girls hugged each other.

Harry came right over. "I never thought I'd outlast Sid or Mary," he said.

"Yeah," I agreed, but I was uneasy about how he'd done it.

Sidney was furious. "I should have

at least been third. *Not you, Harry the canary!"*

"Well, Sid the squid," Harry replied calmly, "you have to concentrate."

"You mean not pay atten-

tion to your *stupid* jokes!" Mary snapped. "I got robbed!"

"All's fair in love and war, Mare," Harry explained.

"Oh yeah?" Mary snarled. "Well, all's fair in love and war for the *other* events too, *Harry Spooger!"* Then she stomped off!

*Whoa*, I thought. *A war?*

Mr. Marks waved us over. "It's getting really warm, kids! Time for a break!"

he shouted. He and Mrs. Cherry were passing out chilled water bottles in a shaded area.

I was glad for some relief! Everyone needed to cool off. As I gulped down some water, I knew I had to keep Harry from any more possible cheating! There would be an all-out war with Sid and Mary if I didn't!

| Team | Points |
|---|---|
| Flying Birds | III |
| Dashing Doorknobs | |
| Star Jumpers | II |
| Speedy Spiders | |
| Rockin' Dudes | I |

# Water Brigade Washout

As we moved on to the second event, I tried to have positive thoughts. We were headed for South School's new nature area. It was shaded and involved more water.

Mrs. Matalata, our art teacher, welcomed us to the water brigade event. She had a flowered scarf tied around her hair and was standing next to a big bucket of water.

"I *love* your T-shirts!" she exclaimed. "What great artists you are!" That put a smile on my face.

"Okay, kids! Let's get started," she said. "In this event, you have to walk across the field with a cup of water. One partner will line up here on my side; the other partner will line up at the other end of the field by Mrs. Michaelsen."

We all waved to Mrs. Michaelsen, our librarian. It was fun to see her in a baseball cap.

Mrs. Matalata continued her instructions. "See how fast you can run over and back without spilling too much water. The first team to finish with no less than six ounces wins!"

Harry patted the water bottle that was hooked on to his belt loop. "I've

come prepared, Dougo!" he said. "This will give us an advantage!"

And that's when my eyeballs zeroed in on Harry's water bottle. The top had a spray trigger! *Oh no!* I thought. Was he planning to squirt extra water into his cup when no one was looking?

As I walked over to the far side, I thought about what I could do.

By the time I got to Mrs. Michaelsen and her card table of filled water cups, I was freaking out. My palms were sweating so much I had to wipe them on my pant legs. When I looked again at my hands, they were shaking.

I took a full cup and went to the starting line. The water inside was beginning to swirl around and around. I could see the black line on the outside of the paper cup for six ounces. The water level was now above it.

When I glanced at my competition, Mary, ZuZu, and Ida were on either side of me. The kid with a doorknob T-shirt was raring to go!

"On your mark . . . " Mrs. Michaelsen called out.

"Get set . . . "

I had to stop Harry from cheating.

"GO!" Mrs. Michaelsen yelled.

Ida and Mary took off like me, walking fast, holding their cup of water out in front of them. ZuZu ran ahead!

As I hurried across the field, my cup

looked like it was attached to a milk-
shake machine. It shook constantly!
Water began sloshing out!

I could hear Harry yelling, "Go! Go!"

By the time I was halfway over to
him, ZuZu had already passed his cup to
Dexter. I was sure Harry would squirt
more water into our cup. The water level
was below the black mark already! Now
there was *no way* we could win.

Unless . . . Harry cheated!

Ida passed her cup to Sidney, who took off like a rocket. Mary gave hers to Song Lee. Song Lee walked swiftly but steady. By the time I got closer to Harry, I was so nervous, I lost my balance and tripped over my own feet! My paper cup landed in the dirt upside down while I did a belly flop onto the grass!

I felt like crying.

"Are you okay?" Harry asked as he dropped to his knees in front of me.

"I'm fine," I groaned.

Harry offered his hand and helped me up. "We'll win the next one," he said.

Then he squirted water in my face. "You need a refresher," he added.

"Thanks," I said as I wiped the dripping water off my cheeks.

*Did I misjudge Harry?* I thought.

Harry watched the rest of the race, and even congratulated the Dashing Doorknobs, who won the event. Dexter and ZuZu finished before them, but their cup had less than six ounces of water. Mary and Song Lee came in second.

"You just earned one point for good sportsmanship, Harry," Mrs. Matalata said. "You didn't complain about not getting a chance to do the water brigade. And you were very understanding to your partner."

Harry flashed a toothy grin while Mary rolled her eyeballs.

"We're going to win, Dougo!" Harry declared.

"We can!" I agreed. *If Harry plays fair!* I thought. I needed to show Harry that we could do that!

As soon as Song Lee and Mary checked the teacher's clipboard, they started jumping!

"We're in first place!" Mary bragged.

Sidney looked at Harry. "Your team and mine may be tied for third, but you're going down, Harry, in the next event!"

Whoa, that didn't sound good.

I knew I had to keep an eye on Sid and Harry. The war was about to begin.

# Relay Revenge

Mr. Deltoid was waiting for us at the next event on the blacktop, where white chalked lanes ended at the fence.

"Welcome to the relay race, kids!" he said. "Listen up! The first person on your team will run up to the fence and back for a distance of one hundred yards. After you tag your partner's hand, your partner will run up and back. Whichever team finishes first wins! The South School record for running two hundred yards is thirty-seven seconds. If you miss the fence, you must go back and touch it. Got it?"

"Got it!" lots of us answered.

I wasn't happy about Sidney and Ida lining up next to us. Sid and Harry were not a good mix right now.

"You run first, Doug," Harry said. "I want to be the anchorman."

"Are you sure?" I replied. I noticed Sid was anchorman too. Leaving those two side by side bothered me.

"Definitely," Harry insisted.

"On your mark," the teacher yelled. I got ready to run.

"Get set!"

I faced the fence, wondering what Harry might be up to. Did he have a plan I didn't know about?

"GO!"

I took off!

My eyes were looking straight ahead at that chain-link fence. The steel wire loops were sparking in the sun. I couldn't wait to touch them so I could turn around and check on Harry!

I could hear him cheering. "WAY TO RUN, DOUGO!"

As I approached the fence, I came in sideways for a landing so that way I

wouldn't lose one second turning around.

*Schwissssssh!*

I hit the chain-link fence and raced back toward the other direction. I could see Harry waiting for me at the finish line! I had to get to him before he did anything stupid to Sidney!

I could see my competition as they raced for the fence. ZuZu had a good lead in second place; Song Lee and Ida followed.

Halfway back, my eyes focused on Harry. His hand was waving at me as he waited for my tag. Sidney was kneeling down doing something.

*Smack!* I slapped his palm, and Harry took off!

Phew! What trouble could he get into now? I had given Harry a really good lead, and he was increasing it.

As I watched Harry accelerate, I noticed his left shoelaces were flapping up and down. I know his shoelaces had been tied before we started the race, so that could only mean . . .

Sidney LaFleur!

*That rat!* He untied Harry's shoe!

Harry started to stumble, then looked at his feet and stopped in his tracks. Furiously, he started retying his left shoe. I counted the seconds it took him to do it.

One Mississippi . . .

Two Mississippi . . .

ZuZu tagged Dexter, who took off in his lane! Seconds later, Sidney followed.

Four Mississippi . . .

Dexter caught up with Harry, then whizzed by him.

Five Mississippi!

Six Mississippi! Dexter was almost at the fence.

Seven . . . Now Sid passed Harry.

At last, Harry lunged forward. His shoe was tied! He was a good fifteen yards behind Dexter, but he was gaining on Sid.

Suddenly, Mr. Deltoid called Dexter's

name. He had missed the fence! Dexter had to stop, turn around, and touch it again. What a break!

Harry easily passed Sid, then approached the fence sideways. He lost no time changing directions.

"GO, HARRY, GO!" I yelled.

Everybody was cheering for their partner except Ida.

Dexter was ten yards ahead of Harry, but Harry was gaining speed!

Then Dexter did what good runners never do. He turned around to see who was behind him.

Harry!

He was sprinting toward him! Sid was farther away.

It was going to be close! Very close!

I stepped aside to give Harry room. ZuZu did the same thing for Dexter.

Both boys shot across the finish line!

"TIE for first!" Mr. Deltoid yelled, and clicked his timer. "Forty-three seconds!"

Dexter and ZuZu high-fived.

Harry and I did a knuckle tap as Sid crossed the finish line.

Mr. Deltoid came over to congratulate us. "That was an amazing run! But next time tie your shoes better!"

Harry nodded. He never tattled on anyone. Not even Sid, who ended up placing second with Ida in the relay race.

"Well, Harry," Mr. Deltoid said. "It was a great race, but you and Doug could have set a new record! That's too bad." He walked away, shaking his head.

When Sidney came over to us, Harry had a few words for him. "Wasn't cool, Sid."

"No, it wasn't," Sid agreed. "My . . . bad," he said, still out of breath. "You could have cracked your skull in two. I'm . . . really sorry."

I shot Sid a look.

Then Harry and I raced over to Mrs. Flaubert and her clipboard.

"We're going to be Room 3B's champs!" Harry said.

Mary folded her arms and glared at Harry. "We'll see about that," she grumbled. "We still have two events left! I may not be the fastest person in Room 3B, but I can sure hit a target with a bean bag!"

The war wasn't over.

# Tug-of-War Tumble

Well, the bean bag toss was a total disaster for us! None of the top-scoring teams earned a point! I was so nervous about the war, I missed all three targets. Harry threw his bags way too hard. They would have been home runs in baseball!

Mary was still talking about the event as we headed over to the nature area.

"There I was," she said, "ready to take a well-planned aim, and just as I toss my bean bag, Harry goes, 'Kaff! Kaff! Kaff!'"

"Mare!" Harry laughed. "I got a tickle in my throat. Coughing is not a crime."

"Well . . . both times, you got a coughing attack *right* when I began to throw! It messed me up!"

"Not the third time, Mare, I didn't cough on your third try," Harry added.

"Well, I was waiting for your cough, and *that* distracted me."

"Your bean bag clung to the side of the board. Just missed the target again."

Mary exhaled like a dragon.

I knew I had to keep an eagle eye on Harry. If we were going to win the last event, it had to be fair and square. No more shenanigans, as my grandma would say.

Mr. Skooghammer, our computer teacher, was waiting for us in the nature area. Since he was wearing shorts, we could see his hairy legs. His red beard and mustache made him the hairiest guy at South School. Although our principal, who was standing next to him, was hairy too, Mr. Cardini had his mustache turned up perfectly on both ends. His T-shirt had a picture of Italy on the front, and the five Olympic rings in blue, black, red, yellow, and green on the back.

"Buongiorno!" Mr. Cardini said. "Welcome to the tug-of-war event. Get a pair of garden gloves from Mr. Skooghammer so your hands won't get rope burn."

Harry squirted some water in his mouth, then in mine. "We want to be last," he said. "Let's get at the end of the line behind Ida and Sid."

I nodded.

We all watched the principal tie a red handkerchief in the middle of the rope. Mr. Skooghammer placed orange cones two yards on either side of it.

"Whichever team pulls the red scarf past their cone wins!" Mr. Skooghammer explained. "You and your partner can earn three points together. Be sure you are on the same side as your partner, though."

Mary suddenly appeared. "I over-reacted about your coughing, Harry," she said. "I'm sorry. I just want to win like you do!"

Harry shrugged. "No problem, Mare."

Then she added, "I notice you guys are both getting a sunburn. I bet you didn't pack sunblock. Here, you can use some of mine."

"Gee, thanks, Mare," Harry said. And he squeezed some lotion into his hand and rubbed it over his lower arms and face.

I did too. "Thanks," I said. I was thrilled those two were making up!

When Mary ran back to the front of the other line, Harry and I got ready.

"On your mark!" Mr. Skooghammer shouted.

Harry and I put our gloved hands firmly around the rope.

"Get set!" Mr. Cardini yelled.

"*PULL!*" both men roared.

As soon as Harry and I grabbed the rope and started to pull, our hands slipped right out of our gloves! We fell backward onto the grassy field while the rest of our team went flying forward.

Harry and I looked up. We both had grass in our hair. Our gloves were on the ground. And the other team was cheering madly, "We won! We won!"

After we picked ourselves up, Sidney came rushing over. "Why did you two let go?"

"We didn't!" Harry objected. "The

rope slipped right out of our hands." Then Harry and I stared at our palms. They were covered with grease.

"How did they get so greasy?" Sid asked.

"THE SUNBLOCK!" Harry and I said in unison.

I slapped the side of my head. *Man*, I thought, *why didn't I see through Mary's sneaky plan!*

I wasn't just tripping over my own feet or missing targets. I was losing my smarts!

"It was Mary!" Sid exclaimed. "I remember now she offered you guys that stuff. I know she wanted to get even with you, Harry, and make you lose. But it's not right she made all the rest of us lose too! *I'm telling!*"

While the winning team was still jumping up and down, Sid stomped over to the principal. Harry and I waited and watched as Sid gave Mr. Cardini an earful of facts. Then the principal made a beeline for Mary and had a few words with her.

Boy, was she stunned! Mary looked like she had swallowed a bug!

"Scuse! Scuse!" Mr. Cardini called out. "Due to certain unfortunate events, we need to do the tug-of-war again!"

While Mary's team groaned, our side got excited. We had another chance!

The principal came over and squirted our hands with hand sanitizer. "Rub them clean, boys." And then he handed us another pair of gloves.

"ON YOUR MARK!" Mr. Skoog-hammer shouted again.

Harry and I grabbed the rope and got a good footing.

"GET SET!"

I was ready to tug with all my might!

"PULL!"

"*Heave ho, guys!*" Harry yelled. And our side started to drag Mary's team our way.

Suddenly, we stopped going backward and were being pulled forward.

Now we were inching toward Mary's side!

"*We can do this, guys!*" Harry yelled. "PULL HARDER!"

Our side stopped inching forward and started hauling the other team our way.

Sid was grunting as he pulled.

"Keep it up!" Harry hollered. Inch by inch we moved the red handkerchief closer to our orange cone.

I could hear Mary screaming, "NO! NO!"

"YES! YES!" Harry and I answered as we yanked the red cloth past our cone.

Mr. Cardini blew his whistle! "We have a winner!" he shouted.

Our team cheered as Harry and I slapped everyone five!

Mary plopped on the ground. She was pooped!

"Magnifico!" Mr. Cardini exclaimed. "Great effort, kids!"

I dashed over and checked our teacher's clipboard. Ida and Song Lee were already there. Mary had lost one point for bad sportsmanship! "Sid lost one too?" I whispered to the girls.

"He did," Ida replied. "I saw him untie Harry's shoe when I was running back to tag him. That was awful. I had to tell the teacher. It just took me a while to do it."

When I looked over at Mary, she was standing with the principal. Sid was there too. "And we'll discuss the consequences later," Mr. Cardini said.

| Team | Points | |
|---|---|---|
| Flying Birds |卌 I | 4 |
| Dashing Doorknobs | III | 3 |
| Star Jumpers | 卌 II - I | 6 |
| Speedy Spiders | 卌 III | 8 |
| Rockin' Dudes | III | 3 |

"The Speedy Spiders are the winners for Room 3B!" Mrs. Flaubert announced. "Congratulations, Harry and Doug!"

Harry and I gave each other a bear hug.

Then Sid and Mary came up to us.

"I'm sorry about the sunblock," Mary said softly. "I think I was desperate."

"If I were in my right mind, Mary," I replied. "I would have said no thank you!"

"And I'm still sorry about that shoe-lace business," Sid chimed in.

"Well," Harry said, "I found out how it feels when someone cheats you out of something. Doug and I could have set a new school record today. But I did mess you guys up during that jump roping and I'm sorry about that. So we're even, okay? Just . . . don't *ever* go near my shoelaces again, Sid, or . . ." Harry held up a fist.

"I promise," Sid said. And he held up a fist too. "Don't *you* tell jokes while I'm jumping rope!"

"Won't happen," Harry agreed.

I felt a *big* sigh of relief. The war with Sid and Mary was over! Harry wasn't a big fat cheater after all. Mary and Sid were!

"We did it, Dougo!" Harry said.

"We did!" I replied. Maybe with a *few* shenanigans, I concluded.

"I can't wait to pick that perfect prize for our class!" Harry exclaimed.

"I can't wait to see it!" I replied.

# The Perfect Prize!

That afternoon, Harry kept watching the minute hand tick away on Room 3B's clock. It was 2:30 p.m. and still no sign of Mr. Deltoid.

Mrs. Flaubert handed out popsicles so the wait wasn't painful for me. There was just one more thing I had to clear up. "Hey, Harry," I asked. "Why did you bring that water bottle to school with the squirt nozzle?"

"If you stay cool, it gives you an advantage! And sometimes, I get an occasional tickle in my throat." Then he flashed his white teeth.

*Harry!* I thought.

"Well, you're right," I added, "I need to stay calm. I can't think straight if I'm freaking out! I really need to keep a cool head!"

"You do!" Harry said, then he squirted me in the face.

"Thanks!" I laughed.

Finally, at three o'clock, Mr. Deltoid came. He was carrying that big brown box. When he let it drop to the ground, it hardly made a sound.

"Harry and Doug, come on up. You boys get to award this last prize to your class."

Everyone cheered and clapped except Harry.

"It's the *last* prize left?" he inquired.

"Yes," Mr. Deltoid replied. "I went by winning score totals. The other room winners had more than eight points. But you guys did a terrific job!"

Harry looked like his cat died.

"The perfect prize is gone then," he moaned. "You can open it, Doug."

"Are you sure?" I said.

Harry nodded.

I lifted the flaps and reached down to the bottom of the box. It was a rolled-up poster.

*Oh man*, I thought. *Probably the five food groups*. What a bummer!

Suddenly, Harry grabbed it. "Wait a minute!" he said, unrolleding the poster.

It was a picture of a HUGE HAIRY BROWN TARANTULA!

Everyone stared at it.

No one said a word.

"The perfect prize for Room 3B!" Harry shouted. "I wonder why nobody else took it first."

Then he ran to the front closet door and held the poster up high. "This hairy beauty will remind everyone in Room 3B that *Spiders* rule!"

It *was* the perfect prize for Harry.

The *only* horrible one in the box!